Based on the TV series *Rugrats*® created by Arlene Klasky, Gabor Csupo,
and Paul Germain as seen on NICKELODEON®

SIMON SPOTLIGHT
An imprint of Simon & Schuster
Children's Publishing Division
1230 Avenue of the Americas
New York, NY 10020

This edition published by Grolier Books.
Grolier Books is a division of Grolier Enterprises, Inc.

ISBN 0-7172-6469-6

Runaway Reptar!

Adapted by Cecile Schoberle
from the Script by Jon Cooksey and Ali Marie Matheson

Illustrated by Sharon Ross
with Philip Felix and Jeffrey Mertz

Simon Spotlight/Nickelodeon

"Are you sure this is where your grampa said we're gonna see the movie?" asked Chuckie.

"I think this is some kinda different movie place," said Tommy. "Sorta like parking-lot movies."

"You dumb babies! This is a drive-in!" said Angelica. She turned on her Cynthia walkie-talkie. "Hey, Susie!" she called. "I got cookies. I'll bet you're eatin' healthy stuff."

Susie and her family were in a van parked next to them. "Actually, I've got fresh brownies," replied Susie.

"Oh, yeah?" said Angelica. She grabbed Dil's lollipop. "I got this lollipop!"

"Give it back, Angelica!" said Tommy.

"Oh, brother! You goody-goodies take the fun out of everything," said Angelica.

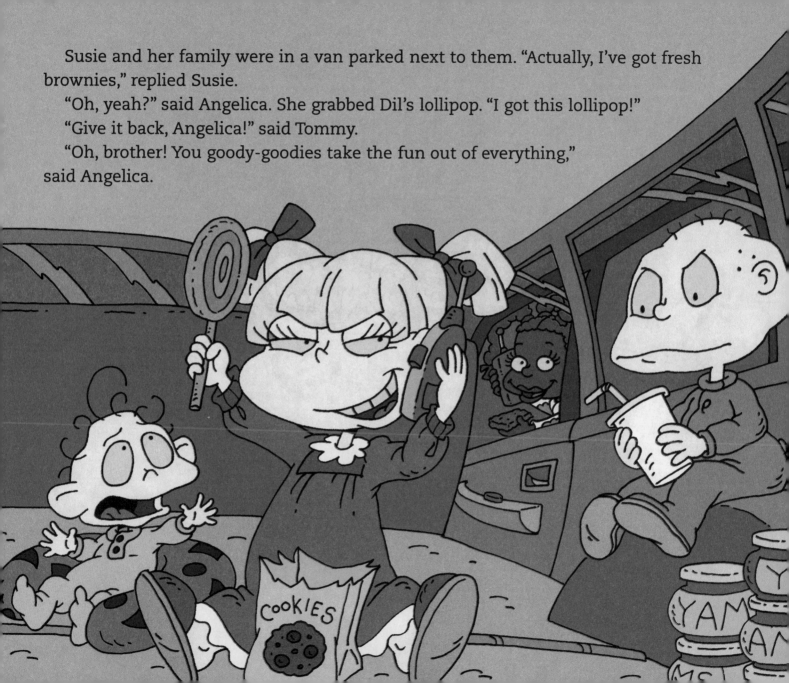

The movie screen flickered. The mighty Reptar roared.

"There he is!" said Phil.

"Reptar's never scared of nothin'," said Chuckie. "He's my hero."

"Oh, he's just a big dumb lizard who likes to smash stuff up," said Angelica.

Just then Dactar appeared. With a loud *screeech!* he flew over Tokyo. The people ran to hide.

"Where's Reptar?" asked Chuckie.

"He's gotta save the people," said Tommy.

Suddenly Reptar rose out of the ocean. "Reptar!" cried the babies.

"This is so dumb," Angelica said.

"Hey, wait a minute. Something's wrong," said Tommy. "Reptar's not beating Dactar up. He's—"

"Helping him!" yelled Chuckie.

"But Reptar's not s'posed to help the bad guy. . . ." said Tommy.

"Ha, ha, ha!" laughed Angelica. "Reptar's turned naughty!"

"There has to be a good reason why he's actin' different," said Tommy. "Maybe he needs a nap or has the sneezles. We gots to go to Pokyo and find out what it is!"

"How are we gonna gets to Pokyo, Tommy?" asked Phil.

"Easy. We'll take my supersecret Reptar car," said Tommy. He pushed a red button.

Suddenly the Reptar wagon rose from the back of Grandpa Lou's car.

"Beep, beep!" said Dil.

"Let's go, guys," said Tommy. "But whatever you do, don't touch that tinkly thing," he warned as he pointed to a knob on the dashboard.

"You comin' with us, Angelica?" he asked.

"Naw, with you babies gone, I'll finally get some peace of quiet . . ." Angelica said, "and all the snacks!"

Tommy fired up the engines of the Reptar wagon, one by one.
Zoom! Off they went!
"Good luck, babies. You'll need it!" Angelica called out.

The babies flew into the movie screen and raced through the empty streets of Tokyo. Suddenly something huge swooped down toward them!

"DACTAAARRR!" the babies screamed.

"Hang on!" yelled Tommy as he swerved the wagon.

Dactar just missed them!

"What if Reptar's mean to us like Dactar?" asked Chuckie.

"Reptar's our hero. We gots to believe in him!" said Tommy.

"I believe that's him eatin' a fire truck," said Phil.

"Tommy, let's go home," said Chuckie, as he poked his hand on a pointy fin of the Reptar wagon. "Ouch!" he yelped.

"Hey, maybe that's the problem," said Tommy. "Maybe Reptar gots a thorn in his paw. If we can pull it out, Reptar will go back to bein' nice."

"How're we gonna see his foot?" asked Phil.

"We'll set a trap so he has to hold still. C'mon!" said Tommy.

Phil and Lil found a barrel of dinosaur treats. Tommy turned on a fire hydrant and made a squishy, sticky mud puddle.

"Good work, guys," said Tommy. "Tasty treats will bring Reptar to our mud puddle fast."

Uh-oh, maybe too fast!

Meanwhile in the Reptar wagon, not too far away, Dil spotted Reptar.

"Doggie," said Dil.

"Doggie?" said Chuckie. "No, Dil, doggies don't . . . breathe fire? Oh, no, Reptar's headin' for Tommy!"

Chuckie raced to save his friend! He scooped Tommy up just in time.

Reptar stomped off and found a refrigerator store. He ripped off the roof.

Clank, clank, clank! Hundreds of magnets quickly flew up and stuck to him.

"How come the forigidater magnets are sticking to Reptar?" Lil asked.

" 'Cause that's not the real Reptar— that's a robot Reptar!" yelled Tommy.

Chuckie gasped. "But who'd wanna build a big robot just to make everybody think Reptar's bein' naughty?"

A wicked laugh rang out.

"Angelica!" said Tommy.

"Why couldn't ya just build somethin' nice?" asked Chuckie.

Angelica frowned. "Because Reptar's a goody-goody, and that bugs me! I figure if I can make the biggest goody-goody of all look terrible, it'll make me look really good."

"And then," Angelica added with a sly smile, "my mommy and daddy will buy me *all* the toys in the store!"

"We're not gonna let you mess up the whole world just so's your mommy and daddy will buy you more toys, Angelica!" declared Tommy.

Angelica laughed. "I'd love to stay," she said, "but I got the whole world to destroy, so I'm off to Mount Fujelica! Seeya-nara!"

The babies gasped.

"We need help!" said Tommy. He punched a button on the Reptar wagon videophone. "Susie?" he called. "Angelica's gonna send out Robot Reptar to mess up the whole world! So we gots to get to Mount Fujelica."

"Okay, we'll keep Robot Reptar busy while you stop Angelica," answered Susie. "Come on," she said to her brothers, "it's time to get dressed."

"How are we gonna get to Mount Fujelica?" asked Phil.

"We'll fly," said Tommy. He pushed another button and wings popped out of the sides. The Reptar wagon lifted high in the air.

Suddenly Chuckie yelled, "It's Dactar! Get movin'!"

The babies flew toward Mount Fujelica. Orange lava
flowed down the mountain.

"How can we get in, Tommy?" asked Lil.

"And what's that stuff?" asked Chuckie.

Dil scooped up some of the lava.

"No, Dilly!" said Tommy.

"Hungry!" Dil said as he ate the orange lava. "Mmm. 'Ams."

"Hey, Dil's right," said Phil, tasting it. "It's mushy yams."

"Okay, hurry, you guys. Eat!" said Tommy. "Dactar's comin'!"

Finally Tommy found a door. The babies entered the volcano.

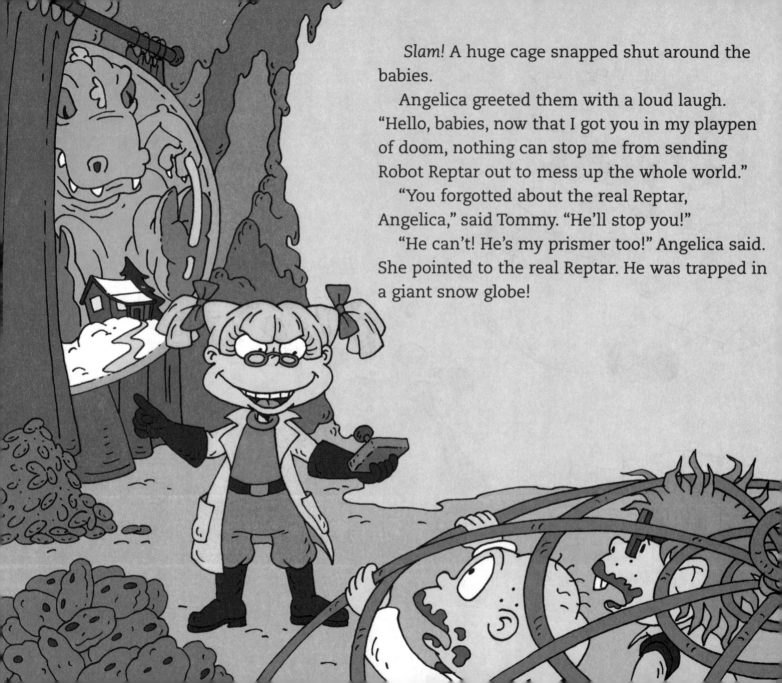

Slam! A huge cage snapped shut around the babies.

Angelica greeted them with a loud laugh. "Hello, babies, now that I got you in my playpen of doom, nothing can stop me from sending Robot Reptar out to mess up the whole world."

"You forgotted about the real Reptar, Angelica," said Tommy. "He'll stop you!"

"He can't! He's my prismer too!" Angelica said. She pointed to the real Reptar. He was trapped in a giant snow globe!

Meanwhile Dil poked at the knob on the dashboard. Then he gave it a good twist.

"No, Dil!" said Tommy. "Not the tinkly thing! Duck, everyone!"

The roof of the Reptar wagon opened. Out came a big dart toy. It fired arrows everywhere! One hit Angelica's control panel.

The babies sneaked out of the cage.

"Uh-oh," said Phil. "I think Dil broke the thingy Angelica uses to tell Robot Reptar what to do."

Crash! Suddenly Robot Reptar broke through the mountain. Susie and her brothers slipped off the robot as it went after Angelica.

"Help!" yelled Angelica.

Tommy quickly jumped into the Reptar wagon and flew around Robot Reptar.

"Nice doggie," said Dil as he tried to pet the robot.

"No, Dil! Not a nice doggie!" said
Tommy.
     It was too late. Robot Reptar snatched
Dil and stomped away!
     "Whee! Ride doggie," said Dil.

"We gots to save Dil!" said Tommy. "But first we gotta let the real Reptar go so he can help us."

Tommy cracked open the snow globe with his screwdriver. Their hero was free!

"We gotta show Reptar we still believe in him," said Tommy. "Okay, Reptar, that robot thingy has my brother Dil. And we need you to get him back. Will you do it?" asked Tommy.

The real Reptar roared and stomped off to find Dil.

"Yay! Go, Reptar, go!" cheered the babies.

The real Reptar chased after the robot Reptar. The robot whirled around. It set Dil down on a nearby skyscraper before fighting off the real dinosaur. The ground shook and buildings fell like toy blocks.

Now Dactar joined in, this time to help the real Reptar!

As the creatures fought, Tommy swooped down in the Reptar wagon and rescued Dil.

The babies cheered as their hero Reptar beat the robot Reptar!

"Dactar's turnin' out to be a hero too!" said Tommy.

"Oh, great. Two goody-goody dinosaurs. At this rate I won't get any new toys until my birthday," said Angelica. "Meddlin' babies!"

"C'mon, guys. Let's go home," said Tommy.

Back in Grandpa Lou's car, Chuckie said, "Gee, Tommy, the world's gonna be okay now!"

"Yeah, it was tough, but we did it," Tommy said as he yawned. "An' you know who helped . . ."

Even in her sleep Angelica knew the answer. "Reptar . . . Reptar . . ." she softly murmured.

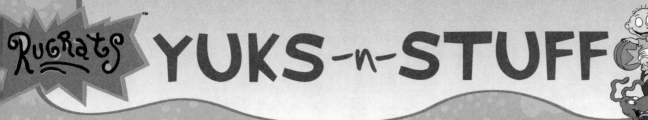

RUGRATS™ YUKS-n-STUFF

Reptar Rules!

Reptar is my favorite monster.
And when I meet him, I will . . .

- Climb up his back to reach the cookies
- Ride him to the park
- Play hide-and-seek
- Ask him about his TV show
- See if he can get tickets to "Reptar on Ice"
- Ask him to help pick up big heavy rocks so Phil and Lil can look for worms underneath
- Make him scare Angelica (just a little!)

Are You a Superhero?

by Tommy

One time my friends thought I was a superhero. I thought maybe I was too. But if any of these are true about you, YOU might really be a superhero!

- You wear a cape.
- You have a secret hideout.
- Your last name is "Man" or "Woman."
- Your name scares bad guys.

- You walk on the ceiling instead of the floor.
- You hide your secret identity by wearing a mask.
- You run so fast, no one can catch you and make you take a bath.

- You fly to your friend's house instead of riding in the car.
- You have enemies with weird names.
- You can lift really big stuff over your head.

- Everything you do ends up in a comic book.
- And every year you get invited to the Superhero's Superparty!